W9-BUB-776

3 1312 00071 3406

Γ⸱

Books by Elizabeth-Ann Sachs

Just Like Always
Where Are You, Cow Patty?
Shyster

SHYSTER

SHYSTER

by
Elizabeth-Ann Sachs

Illustrations by
Judith Gwyn Brown

ATHENEUM 1985 NEW YORK

Library of Congress Cataloging in Publication Data

Sachs, Elizabeth-Ann.   Shyster.

SUMMARY: Becky's experience in owning a cat helps
her in dealing with the departure of her father and
the new man in her mother's life.
1. Children's stories, American. [1. Divorce—
Fiction. 2. Cats—Fiction] I. Title.
PZ7.S1186Sh   1985   [Fic]   85-7943
ISBN 0-689-31161-3

Published simultaneously in Canada by
Collier Macmillan Canada, Inc.
Type set by Heritage Printers, Inc., Charlotte,
North Carolina
Printed and bound by Fairfield Graphics, Fairfield,
Pennsylvania
Designed by Mary Ahern
First Edition

PART I

CHAPTER 1

The view from Becky's room was of the city.
Becky loved to lie on her bed with her elbows on
the windowsill. Sometimes she watched the pigeons who perched on the fire escape. Sometimes,
in between the tall brick buildings, she could see
tugs and barges on the river.

Many mornings she would think, maybe today her father would get off one of those boats
and walk up the street. Every time a man with
dark wavy hair hurried by, she would hope it was
him.

"Becky," her mother called from the other
bedroom. "Are you dressed yet?"

Becky rolled over and sat up. She had washed her face and rebraided her long brown hair even though she hadn't felt like it. But the new red shorts her mother had made, Becky put back in the drawer. She didn't want to look nice.

"Why don't you go downstairs and wait for Arthur." Becky's mother came into the small room. "He should be here any minute."

Mrs. Rader's short brown hair was still damp from the shower. Becky liked how it twisted up into little curls when it was wet. But Becky didn't want her mother to use extra make-up or look pretty for dates with Arthur.

"Momma, can't I stay here? I don't want to go see Arthur's old house in the country."

"I wouldn't leave you home alone all day; you know that. And besides, Arthur invited you especially."

"But suppose Daddy . . ." Becky paused.

"Honey." Becky's mother lifted her chin. "You know that Daddy isn't going to turn up."

Becky sighed. It had been over a year since they had heard from her father. First he'd stopped writing notes with the money he sent. Then he stopped sending the money he'd promised. Even if her parents were divorced, it was still hard for Becky to believe that he would just go off and forget her. Sometimes she pretended he was sick in a faraway hospital. But her mother said it wasn't likely.

Mrs. Rader gave Becky a hug. "Why don't you take the picnic basket down to the front stoop. Arthur will put it in the car."

Instead of taking the elevator, Becky decided to walk down the stairs. She liked to look out the window on each landing.

From the third floor, Becky could see the tarred roofs of other buildings. At the second story window, she saw a lady watching television in her living room and a cat sleeping on a ledge. Finally, on the first floor, Becky looked out on a busy city street.

Her father had shown her that trick a long time ago, and Becky had never forgotten it. When she stood in front of each window, she tried to pretend he was with her, but it made her miss him even more.

Outside, Becky sat on the concrete steps and continued studying the brick building. Iris, who was going into fourth, same as Becky, lived on the first floor. But Iris and her family had gone to the shore for the summer. There weren't any other kids on the block, except Susan, and she was only in kindergarten.

Next, Becky watched a party of ants climbing over one another to get to a heap of ice cream that someone had dropped. The plop was melting, and a long chocolate trickle inched toward the curb. A scrawny black cat slipped out from under a parked car. With his tail in the air, he stood eyeing the ice cream.

Becky watched the cat's pink tongue scrape the sidewalk. It made a scratching sound. When he was done, the cat sat on his haunches and washed his face.

"Are you hungry?"

The cat looked at Becky and yawned a wide-open-mouth yawn.

"My mother says you're supposed to cover your mouth when you do that, cat. Where are your manners?" Becky moved down to the next step.

The cat only blinked and looked over his shoulder.

She opened the picnic hamper. "I'm sure old Arthur Myers won't miss a little chicken." Becky peeled off a piece.

The cat sniffed the air, watching her. He didn't move.

Becky threw a small hunk onto the sidewalk

halfway between herself and the cat. "Go on," she coaxed. "Take it."

The cat lowered his head, sniffing. Standing, he stretched first his front legs, then his back. He moved over to the meat, slowly.

Becky watched him gobble it up. He's starving, she thought, throwing him another piece. The cat had to be one of the strays that she heard fighting or knocking over garbage cans in the alley.

He looked at Becky, for more.

"You'll have to come get it." Becky leaned over and put the meat on the bottom step.

The cat didn't move. He stared at Becky and then down the street.

"Come on," Becky said. "Come and get it." She tapped her finger on the stone step.

The black cat inched up the outside of the stairs beyond the metal railing. He stuck his head between the rusty bars but wouldn't come through. Becky picked up the pieces and extended her hand. The cat's rough tongue scraped against her fingers when he snatched the meat. He gulped it, then disappeared into the bushes.

"That was really something," a voice behind Becky said. "You've got a nice way with animals."

There stood tall, skinny Arthur in his plaid slacks and pink shirt. He was giving Becky his goofy smile.

"Hello, Arthur."

"Is your mother ready yet?" He leaned on the black railing.

"I'll go see." Becky stood. "She said you should put this in the car."

Becky handed over the basket and started up the three flights of stairs. She didn't want to think about Arthur Myers or count the number of times her mother had gone out with him. Becky wanted her father to come back soon.

CHAPTER 2

After breakfast the next morning, Becky slipped
two cold sausages wrapped in a paper towel into
her pocket. All during the picnic at Arthur's she
had thought about the black alley cat. "Momma,
you know what I need?" Becky picked up a dishtowel to dry the cereal bowls. "I need a pet."

"Oh, honey, we don't really have the room.
We're just about bursting out of this apartment
now. Why don't you wait until we move?" Mrs.
Rader wiped down the counter with a sponge.

"I was thinking of a small one, like a cat."

"Where would we keep the litter box? And

how would we let him in and out? The downstairs doors are all locked."

Becky had spent the whole ride back from the country thinking over what her mother would say about a pet. "We could keep the litter box in the bathroom near the sink, and I would take real good care of him. Momma, say yes."

Mrs. Rader smiled at Becky. "I'd really rather wait until we decide where we're moving."

"But, Momma, there's this kitten in the alley. Someone else might take him."

"A stray!"

"Why not?"

"He could be diseased from living in the streets."

"I fed him some chicken, yesterday. He looked really hungry to me, and he loved your chicken, Momma."

"Now, how could I possibly turn away a cat who liked my fried chicken!"

"Does that mean yes?"

"I want to get a look at him, first."

"Yea," yelled Becky, throwing the dishtowel into the air.

Mrs. Rader caught the towel. "We still have to decide about moving to Arthur's house."

Becky made a face that her mother didn't

notice. Mrs. Rader was busy folding up the cloth.

When they took the garbage out, Becky and her mother searched the back alley. They found the young black cat snoozing near the side of the brick building where the sun was shining.

"Isn't he a beauty?" Becky squeezed her mother's hand.

"He's a sack of bones, Becky."

"Don't say that. You'll hurt his feelings."

Mrs. Rader shook her head. "Sometimes you remind me of your father."

"What do you mean?"

"He was always picking up strays, too."

"I didn't know that. Now I really want him."

The cat sat up on his hind legs. He made a purring rumble as Becky stooped over.

"See, he even remembers me." She placed the sausage before him.

The cat batted the sausage with his paw. Then he settled into his meal.

"Becky, our apartment is just too small for an animal, especially one who is used to running free—"

"But Momma!" Becky interrupted. She looked up at her mother's serious face.

"—If we had a whole lot of room, like at Arthur's house, it would be easier."

"You mean I can't have a pet unless I live with *him*?"

"I'm not saying that. You can have a pet. I'm just not sure about this one. A goldfish or a parakeet might be better."

Becky looked at the skinny cat chewing on a piece of sausage. "But I want him."

"He's wild, Becky. He'll hate not being able to come and go as he pleases."

Becky sat on the ground near the garbage cans. "Maybe he'll like being indoors. You don't know."

Mrs. Rader crouched beside Becky, watching the cat. "It's not likely, but I guess we could try it. However, if he doesn't adjust, you just cannot keep him."

"Oh, Momma!" Becky hugged her mother. "I know it'll work!"

"Well, we'll see. There are some other things to think about also."

Becky frowned. "Like what?"

"He might actually belong to someone."

Becky shook her head. "He couldn't; he lives out here."

"We should make sure. You wouldn't like it if someone suddenly adopted your pet."

"I guess not."

"You could ask the man who sweeps the halls in our building. He'll know if the cat belongs to anyone."

"Okay," said Becky.

"And I'll put a sign on the bulletin board at the grocer's. If no one shows up in a few days, then we'll ask a vet what he thinks."

"Do we have to wait that long?"

"It's only fair."

Becky petted the cat's head. "I want to find the janitor right now."

CHAPTER 3

Three days later, Becky's mother stopped the car for a red light. They were on the way home from the vet's. The streets of the city were crowded with cars, bicyclists and people. Becky sat in the front seat with the black cat in a box. He was trying to scratch his way out.

"What should I call him?" Becky peered through one of the holes in the side.

"Wait awhile and see what he's like." Mrs. Rader turned the corner and pulled down their street. "Oh, good, there's a parking space."

Becky carried the box into the apartment building. The cat scratched at the cardboard as they waited for the elevator. "It's okay," she told him.

Mrs. Rader pushed the elevator button again. "It's hard to believe," she said when the doors opened, "that he could be almost a year old. He must have been nearly starving to death."

"Aren't you glad we got him, Momma?"

"I don't know yet, Becky."

Becky opened the box on the living room floor. The cat jumped out and disappeared under the couch. "Come out here, cat."

"Now remember what the vet said. He's probably never been indoors. You have to give him time." Mrs. Rader dropped a bulky brown shopping bag on the counter.

Becky followed her mother into the kitchen. "You think I should feed him?"

"How about water? And then you can fix up the litter box."

"Okay." Becky took the blue plastic box out of the grocery bag.

"After that you can set the table. Arthur is coming for dinner."

Bor-ing, Becky said to herself. At least she'd have the cat to play with while her mother and Arthur sat talking. "Does he like cats, Momma?"

"I know he loves dogs." Mrs. Rader carried

the ten-pound bag of litter into the bathroom.

"Well, he better like my cat," Becky yelled from the kitchen. She placed the metal bowl of water under the table where the cat could find it.

All afternoon, Becky tried to coax the cat out from under the couch with a play mouse on a piece of string. He was still hiding after dinner.

"He'll come when he's good and ready." Arthur smiled across the table at Becky. "You won't be able to get rid of him. You'll see."

Becky said nothing. She didn't like the way Arthur pretended to know everything about everything just because he was a teacher. She carried her dish into the kitchen.

"But I do know one cat trick that might work," Arthur said.

Becky blasted the dishes in the sink with hot water. Another one of Arthur Myers's dumb ideas, she thought.

"There isn't a cat," Arthur said, coming into the kitchen—he opened a narrow drawer—"who can resist a foil ball."

Becky squished liquid soap on the dishes. *Oh sure*, she thought. She wasn't even going to watch.

But out of the corner of her eye, Becky saw Arthur wad up three fat silver balls. He threw one near the leg of the couch. A long, furred arm appeared and swatted it.

"Becky, come and look at this." Her mother laughed.

Becky dried her hands. She said nothing to Arthur, but took the other silver balls when he offered them to her. She stretched out on her stomach and shot one under the couch. The cat batted it back at her and stuck out his head.

"He's pretty tricky." Mrs. Rader poured herself more iced tea.

"Do it across the rug," Arthur suggested.

Quit telling me what to do, Becky thought. She shot a ball in front of the cat's nose and toward the radiator. The cat pounced after the foil ball. She did it again, and this time he disappeared behind the desk.

Becky played with the cat, forgetting about her mother and Arthur, while they cleaned up the dishes. When they went out for a breath of cool air on the front stoop, she stayed behind.

The cat chased the ball into her room and squeezed in under the bed. He stayed there.

Becky lay down on the floor with her head pressed against the cold metal bedrail. She could see the black heap curled up near her old sandals.

"I wish you'd stop hiding. You don't have to be afraid of me."

Becky heard him purring. Well, at least, she thought, he likes my voice. "I don't know why my mother keeps going out with goofy Arthur. Just because they're both teachers. What's so great about that? Arthur's nowhere near as good-looking as my father. And Arthur thinks he's so smart. I bet my father knows more than he does."

The purring deepened. Against his own blackness, the cat's eyes were like shiny yellow marbles.

"You'd like my father, cat. He used to tell me neat stories about sleeping in the woods. I bet dumb old Arthur doesn't know a thing about that."

"Becky?" her mother called from the living room.

"In here, Momma."

"What are you doing in the dark?"

"Talking to my cat."

"Arthur said to say 'so long'." Mrs. Rader sat on the rug. She unbuckled her sandals.

Becky didn't answer.

"How's the cat doing?"

"Fine. I really want to think of a name for

him." She moved over and rested her head on her mother's leg.

"How about something like Midnight or Blacky? That's what he reminds me of."

"Could I call him Shy 'cause he won't come out from under the bed?"

"Or shy-ster."

"What's a shyster?"

"Someone who's sneaky or tricky." Her laughter filled the darkness. "Someone who hides under couches."

Becky sat up. "Hey, I like that." She tried out the name. "Shyster, here, Shyster."

There was no movement from under the bed. Even the purring had stopped.

"Well, Becky." Mrs. Rader lifted herself off the rug. "It's time you were in bed."

"Can Shyster sleep with me?"

"If you promise not to fool around all night."

"We won't." Becky kicked off her sneakers. "I won't even read."

"You don't have to go that far." Mrs. Rader leaned over and kissed Becky.

After the door closed, Becky undressed. She changed into her father's old t-shirt, the one she liked to sleep in, and went to brush her teeth.

When she came back, Becky found Shyster sitting in the window. She stretched out on the bed with her elbows on the wide sill beside him.

A stiff, hot breeze was blowing up from the river. She could smell the water. A barge lined with green and yellow lights floated by.

Down below, a garbage can fell over. Someone shouted. A cat yowled.

Becky watched Shyster sniff the breeze. It seemed to her he was reading the darkness. Shyster paced the width of the window and curled up in the other corner of the sill.

Becky watched the river with him. When she could keep her eyes open no longer, she crawled under the covers and fell asleep.

It didn't feel as if she had been asleep very long, but something awakened her. Becky sat up.

In the moonlight, she saw the small black cat with his face and front paws pressed against the screen. He whined, then paced the window sill.

"Shyster, what's wrong?"

The cat dropped on all fours. He concentrated his attention on something outside.

Becky laughed when she looked out onto the fire escape. There were several gray pigeons huddled together on the railing.

Shyster's back end wiggled. His tail shook. He whined as he got ready to pounce against the screen.

"Come on, you dumb cat." Becky scooped him up. "You can't do that." With the other hand she shut the window.

Shyster grumbled and jumped from her arms. Becky thought she saw him disappear under her bed.

For a long time Becky lay awake thinking about Shyster trying to catch a pigeon. She was just drifting off to sleep when she heard the crash.

"Becky?" Her mother called from the other bedroom. "Are you all right?"

Before there was hardly time to answer, the light flashed on in her room. "Becky, what happened?"

Becky rubbed her eyes with a fist. "It must have been Shyster."

"Where is he?"

"I don't know."

"I'm going to find out what that noise was."

Becky followed her mother into the living room. One of the ceramic flower pots had fallen from the window ledge. Dirt and pottery and plants lay scattered all over the rug. There was no cat to be seen.

"What a mess!" Mrs. Rader began picking up the pieces.

Becky went into the kitchen for the dustpan and broom. When they were almost done cleaning, she said, "Shyster knocked it over. I saw him throwing himself at the screen in my room. He was trying to catch pigeons on the fire escape."

Mrs. Rader nodded. "I see."

"I closed the window in my room, and he must have come in here."

"Well, let's go back to bed." Mrs. Rader turned Becky around by the shoulders. "It's late."

But when Becky was tucked in, her mother sat on the edge of the bed. "Maybe we should talk now, before we both get too attached to that silly cat. Becky, I'm afraid he's not going to work out for us."

"Momma, can't we just see what happens for the next few days?"

Mrs. Rader shook her head. "Becky, this

place is just too cramped. I think a smaller pet would be better."

"If we moved to a bigger apartment, we could keep him."

"Yes, but we aren't going to move to a bigger apartment."

"Well, I *don't want* to live with Arthur!"

"Becky, you can't always have your own way. Sometimes it's necessary to give in."

Becky was quiet. What her mother said was hard to understand.

"Tell me why you don't want to live with him."

"He's no fun," Becky blurted out. "Not like Daddy, anyway."

"I know you think that, but I wish you'd get to know him a little. Arthur's a really good person."

"But he can't hunt deer or live in a cave like Daddy."

"Did you ever ask him?"

"No." Becky sat up. She didn't like the idea of Arthur telling her stories the way her father used to. "What if Daddy comes home? If we go away, he won't know where we are."

"Honey, he's not going to."

"Can't we just move without Arthur?"

"No, Becky. We can't afford it. Besides, I really want to try living with him."

"You don't want to marry Arthur, do you?"

"He's my friend, but I'm not sure about marrying right away."

Leaning forward, Becky put her head on her mother's shoulder. She felt scared inside.

"I'll tell you what," Mrs. Rader said. "Let's try it for the month of August and just see what happens. It will sort of be like a vacation."

"Will Arthur let me bring Shyster? If we go, can I keep him?"

"Of course, and Shyster can roam around all he wants. Arthur also said there's a girl up the road you might like."

"Can I call Granny and tell her where we're going in case Daddy does come back?"

"If you want to."

"And we can come home if I hate it?"

"Yes, if you really, really hate it."

"Okay," said Becky, "I'll try then."

PART 2

CHAPTER 4

"Do I have my own room?" Becky asked her mother when they were unpacking the car at Arthur's.

"I don't know yet, honey." Mrs. Rader shifted her sewing machine from one hand to the other, then picked up a suitcase. "Why don't you ask?"

Becky shut the car door with her foot. In her arms, Shyster squirmed, but she didn't put him down. "It's okay," Becky whispered into the cat's soft black fur.

Inside, the house was dark and quiet. There

was a clock ticking somewhere. "Arthur, where are you?"

"On the second floor, Becky."

Becky carried Shyster up the narrow carpeted stairs. Every step had is own creak.

From the landing, Becky looked down the shadowy hallway at the row of doors. "Arthur?" she said again.

"At the end of the hall."

Becky moved along the red and green flowered wallpaper, past an old-fashioned maroon couch. She paused in front of the only door that was slightly ajar.

"Come on in." Arthur opened the door.

The sunshine surprised Becky when she stepped into the small room. Bright light filled the lace curtains and made patterns on the yellow walls. A bed was tucked into one corner where the ceiling slanted down. And someone had put flowers in a jar on the desk.

"Whose room is this?"

"Do you like it?" Arthur jiggled the latch on the window.

"It's really pretty."

"Then it's all yours."

"Thanks," Becky said, putting Shyster on the white spread. She sat down, too.

Meanwhile Arthur pounded on the window with his fist. He was trying to get it open. Becky knew her father would have been strong enough to just shove the window up. It made her miss him. "Ahh," said Arthur when the window finally gave. "I thought I had this open last summer."

Becky noticed the pictures on the wall. "Does this room belong to someone?"

Arthur looked out at the view. When he turned back, he said, "It was my sister's."

"Will she mind me using it?"

Arthur hesitated, then said, "I'm sure she'd love to know you were."

"I won't let Shyster mess things up here." Becky petted the cat.

"You should let Shyster out." Arthur picked up his tool chest. "He'll love the woods."

Becky frowned. "I can't do that yet. Suppose he gets lost?"

Arthur chuckled. "Cats don't get lost. They know their way around by instinct. He could get back to the city if he wanted to."

Becky closed the door to her room. Was Arthur telling the truth? "Hey, Shyster!" Becky sat on the bed. "Can you show me the way home?"

After lunch, Becky's mother said, "The unpacking can wait." She folded in the milk carton spout. "Why don't we take that walk now?"

Arthur swallowed his coffee. "Good. I was afraid you'd start sewing and never see the view."

"That's why I want to get outdoors first." Mrs. Rader smiled at Arthur.

Becky pushed back her chair. "Well, I'll see you later."

"You sure you won't come with us, honey?"

"I'm staying with Shyster."

Arthur stood up. "He'll probably want to be outside, too."

Becky shook her head.

"Will you be all right alone?" Mrs. Rader asked.

"Sure, she will." Arthur winked at Becky.

Pretending not to see him. Becky pushed in her chair. She heard the porch door slam. From the window over the sink, Becky watched her mother and Arthur cross the road. They stood in front of the stone wall, then they climbed it and started into the field.

"Shyster? Where are you, pal?" Becky wandered through the dark, stuffy living room and out to the hallway. She opened the front door.

Outside, the summer wind hissed in the trees, and birds sang afternoon songs. The road at the end of Arthur's yard ran up a hill and twisted out of sight near the mountains.

There was a rumbling sound off in the distance, and Becky waited to see what it was. A blue pickup truck roared around the curve. A girl with blond hair and a big dog sat in the open back. The girl waved to Becky.

Becky didn't wave back. There was a cloud of dust and silence after the truck rushed out of sight. Even if the country was as pretty as her father said, Becky wished she'd stayed at the apartment.

A warm, furred body rubbed against Becky's leg. Shyster whined.

"Let's see if you really can find the city." Becky picked him up and tried to unlatch the screen door with one hand.

The cat jumped out of her arms. He landed on all fours with a thud.

"Come here, Shyster." Becky stepped toward him.

Shyster turned and started into the kitchen. He stopped and waited in the doorway for Becky.

"What is it, cat?" She paused halfway down the hall.

Shyster came back and circled her legs.

"Arthur doesn't know what he's talking about. You can't show me how to get back if you won't even go outdoors!"

The cat walked beside Becky heading her toward the kitchen.

"Are you still hungry? I just fed you." Becky laughed. Ever since they'd adopted him, Shyster had done nothing but eat. Becky fed the cat whenever he begged.

Shyster settled in front of the empty blue bowl. He wrapped his black paws around the base. Blinking his yellow eyes, he watched as Becky opened a cabinet door.

"Nope, not in there," she teased.

Shyster sat up when Becky pulled out the big checkered bag of treats. He whined again.

"Here you go." She dumped a handful in front of him.

The cat settled into chewing.

"You still haven't learned to say thank you." Becky stroked the top of his flat black head. "But at least you're not as skinny anymore."

Shyster didn't look up until he was finished. And then he wanted more.

"Hey, cat." Becky slipped Shyster extra treats. "You're going to get fat."

CHAPTER 5

Becky spent several days helping her mother unpack. Mrs. Rader picked out a sunny room on the second floor for sewing. Together they refolded material to fit on the book shelves next to the sewing machine. And Becky spent one whole day sorting buttons, then putting them in little clear plastic drawers.

Finally, there was nothing more to do except to stack the spools of colored thread in the sewing box. Becky liked to see all the blues in one corner and greens in another.

"I have to get working," Mrs. Rader said,

"or neither of us will have anything new when school starts."

They heard the screen door slam downstairs, then footsteps in the front hall. "Becky are you ready?"

Becky looked down at the red and pink spools of thread. She didn't want to go out with Arthur.

Mrs. Rader smiled. "Go on. You'll have a good time."

"But I'd rather stay with you."

"I'll be busy cutting out material. You'll have fun."

Arthur came through the door. "All set?"

Becky followed him downstairs. On the porch, Shyster snoozed in an old armchair near the window. Arthur waited with the screen door open while Becky petted the cat. "I tried to get him outside the day we got here," Becky said. "But he only wanted to eat."

Arthur smiled. "I think Shyster can't get over his good fortune. He gets whatever he wants."

Becky thought then that Shyster really could have lived in their apartment, but she didn't say it. She just knew he didn't care about being outdoors.

"Maybe you should get another cat," Arthur suggested.

"What for?"

"If Shyster had a buddy they could play together."

"Maybe he just likes being in the city better," Becky said.

Outside it was growing muggy. Crickets hidden in the tall grass sang about the heat. Arthur led the way around the side of the house and passed the old apple tree under her bedroom window.

The woods were cool and shadowy when they stepped into them. "Have you ever seen fresh animal tracks?" Arthur stopped near a small stream.

"Only in an old scouting book of my father's." Becky bent down alongside him. The muddy ground was pressed with all size prints.

"Is this mouse?" She pointed to a small set.

"Yes." Arthur sounded surprised. "How did you know?"

"That little line in between the footprints. My father said mice and rats drag their tails."

"Very good!" Arthur said.

In spite of herself, Becky was pleased. If

only her father could know how many things she'd learned, just like him.

Arthur crossed the stream, stepping from rock to rock. "I'd like to see that book sometime. Sounds like a good one."

Unsteadily, Becky moved from one mossy stone to another. She concentrated on her feet, not knowing what to say. Sharing the book with Arthur would be like giving her father away.

When they came to a clearing, the sun beat down on them again. Arthur cut across the grassy field. There were horses gathered under a cluster of trees.

"We came by the shortcut to Ryan's farm. Ryan and I have been using it since we were kids." Before them was a white farmhouse with a barn tucked behind it. A girl came across the yard driving a small red tractor. "Hi, Mr. Myers," she shouted over the roar. She jolted to a stop, killing the noise.

"Hello, there," Arthur called. "Martha was in my third grade this year," he said.

Becky watched the girl with curly blond hair climb off the tractor. She was tall and very tan. It was the same girl who had waved when they first came.

"Hi, I'm Martha. You have to be Becky."

"Yes," said Becky. There was something about the glow on Martha's wide face that made Becky think of an angel.

"I saw you in Mr. Myers's—I mean Arthur's doorway. I'm the one who waved."

"I didn't know who you were."

"That's what I thought. I've been waiting for you to come over."

"You've been waiting for me?" Becky said, surprised.

"Yeah, I've been waiting all summer really."

"I told the Ryans you might be coming," Arthur said, quickly.

Becky laughed, not knowing what to say. "Where's your dad, Martha?"

"Out in the pasture with the foal." Martha pointed towards the field.

"Have a good time, you two," Arthur called over his shoulder. "I'll see you later, Becky."

"Arthur told me all about you before school ended. I've been dying for you to come. There aren't any girls my age close by. Have you ever been on a farm before?"

Becky watched Arthur disappear behind the house. "No." She turned to Martha. "Only a pretend one at the zoo."

"Come on then, I'll show you around."

"Okay." Becky matched strides with Martha as they started for the dirt drive.

Inside, the white stone barn was cool and empty. The cement floor was covered with straw. Becky leaned over a metal divider. "What are these things for?"

"Each one of the stalls usually has a cow in it. But they're all outside for the summer. We only bring them in to be milked."

Becky followed Martha to the other end of the building. In the doorway, a cat who was almost as black as Shyster sat washing a paw. Another red-haired one ran outside. Becky squatted down. "Here kitty," she said holding out two fingers for the cat to sniff.

"That's Hades, one of our barn cats. She has a huge litter of kittens. The other one was Leda. She's going to have babies, too."

"How many cats do you have?"

"I don't know exactly. My father wants lots around to kill mice. Only now he says we have way too many."

"Could I see the kittens?"

"Sure, but they're nothing special."

Martha put her hands in her back pockets as she walked. "Barn cats mostly live outdoors on whatever they kill and any cow milk we give them."

"My cat, Shyster, lived in an alley and ate whatever people threw away."

"In the city?"

"Yes."

"Huh." Martha laughed. "City cat and country cat."

Becky smiled. She put her fingers in her back pockets and walked along with Martha.

Hades, Martha told Becky, had hidden her kittens under the stairs in the Ryans' basement. No one was sure how she had gotten into the house or when exactly she had had them.

"They're about five or six weeks old." Martha knelt down near the heap of fur under the stairs. There were two grays, two spotted and one black. "My father wants to get rid of this litter. With Leda's kittens coming, we'll be overrun."

Becky took the gray striped kitty that Martha handed her. "What'll you do with him?"

Martha shrugged. "I don't know yet. Nobody around here needs cats."

"Maybe I could take one. Arthur said I should get another cat to keep Shyster company."

"Isn't he great?"

"He's a neat kitten."

"No, Mr. Myers—I mean Arthur."

"Oh."

"All the kids at school love him. He's the best teacher. He even said I should call him Arthur when we're not at school."

"He's my mother's friend." Becky patted the warm ball in her lap. "Does the kitten have a name?"

"I've been calling him Toby."

"Want to come home with me, Toby?" Becky stroked the kitten's head. Toby purred, curling up in Becky's lap.

"Come on," said Martha, "I want to show you my horse."

"Toby can go with you in a week or so," Martha said to Becky late that same day. They were standing at the edge of the woods.

"I'd better ask my mother before I promise to take him. Can we get together tomorrow?"

"Sure, if you want to."

"Yeah, I do if you do."

Martha laughed. "I'll see you, then." She turned to leave.

"Great." Becky started toward the thick

brush and dense trees. "Hey Martha, is this the path I take? I don't know how to go."

Martha came back. "I forgot. I'll walk you part way."

It was twilight in the woods. Little brown chipmunks scurried back and forth across the trail. When they came to the stream, Martha stopped.

"Just stay on the path. You can see Arthur's house when you get around that big rock up there."

"Today was fun."

"For me too. I'm glad you're not real awful." Martha laughed.

"What do you mean?" Becky said puzzled.

"I kept worrying that you might be snobby. That's why I asked Arthur."

"Martha, would you tell me something?"

"What?"

"What did he say about me?"

Martha leaned against a tree. She crossed her feet at the ankles and looked at the ground. "He said you might come to live with him, but he wasn't sure."

"Anything else?" Becky kicked over a rock in the stream.

Martha shifted her position, and a serious

look came over her face. "One night I heard him talking to my father and mother. They were out on the porch, and I was supposed to be asleep. See, my room is right over where they were sitting and I—"

"What did he say?" Becky interrupted.

"That your father had disappeared and . . ." Martha hesitated.

"And what?"

"And that you were sad."

"He said that?"

"Arthur said it was a real hard thing."

"How would he know?"

Martha shrugged. "I don't know, but my mother said Arthur's sister died when he was little."

"She's dead! That's whose room I'm sleeping in!"

"Is it spooky?"

Becky shrugged. "Not really."

"No ghosts or anything?"

"I never saw one. I wonder why he didn't tell me."

"Maybe he thought you'd get scared. Could I see it sometime?"

"Yeah, sure. Well, thanks." Becky crossed the shallow stream. "See you tomorrow."

"Come early. If you can," Martha called over her shoulder.

"I will," Becky yelled.

Arthur and Mrs. Rader were shucking corn under the trees in the back yard when Becky decided to ask. "Would it be all right if I got a friend for Shyster?"

"What do you mean, a friend?" Becky's mother made a funny face.

"Arthur said it might be good for Shyster to have a buddy." Becky looked at Arthur.

He nodded.

"Well, I don't know, Becky. You haven't had Shyster that long."

"I know, but there's this real cute kitten over at Martha's. They've got too many."

Arthur wrapped the corn husks and silk in a brown bag. "I'll go dump this in the garbage." He headed across the lawn.

"Is it okay with you, Momma?"

"If you take care of it, I guess it'll be all right."

"I will."

"Oh, wait a minute! What am I saying?

Becky, if we go back to the city, an extra cat is out of the question. We don't have room for one let alone two. Let's wait till after we decide about that."

"Aww," Arthur said, as he returned. "I'll need a cat around here if you two leave."

Mrs. Rader looked at Arthur and smiled. "Thanks."

"Yeah, thanks," Becky echoed. "I think you'll like him."

"Don't thank me," Arthur said. "You'll have to look after him, Becky, and kittens are a pain."

Becky watched him pile the ears of corn on a platter. *Sometimes*, she thought, *Arthur could be okay.*

CHAPTER 6

Becky stood on the bottom step of the Ryans' porch with the gray kitten in her arms. "Can you come over after supper, Martha?"

"If the weeding's finished."

"Great," said Becky. "See you."

"Hey," Martha shouted.

Becky turned around. "What?"

"Thanks for helping with the chores."

"It was neat." Becky started for the woods.

"Wait till Shyster sees you, little guy." Becky carried the kitten in a blanket like a baby. He shut his green eyes and purred.

During the past week Becky and Martha had

used the path a lot. Martha had taught her how to steal eggs from the chickens, even though the stench in the coop was sickening. And the first time Becky had gone in alone, it had been scary. It was hard to believe that chickens could look so mean.

Now Becky stepped easily from one rock to another at the stream. She didn't even stop to check for tracks.

When she came up the front walk at Arthur's, Becky heard the sewing machine running. "Momma, I'm home," she yelled. "Come meet Toby."

Becky put the kitten down on the armchair where Shyster usually slept. He looked tiny to Becky, standing in the other cat's place.

"Oh, how cute!" Becky's mother came into the room. She kneeled before the chair. "He's like the Cheshire cat in *Alice in Wonderland*. He looks like he's smiling."

Becky beamed. "Where's Shyster?"

"In your room, I think." Mrs. Rader stroked the kitten's white underchin while he purred.

Arthur came in. "Well, well," he said, "our newest member."

They were all gathered around the kitty when Shyster appeared. He rubbed his black body up against Becky's legs. Then he noticed the kitten.

His snarl startled Becky. She had never seen a cat with its mouth drawn back and fangs bared.

Shyster's tail twitched from side to side, angrily. He jumped into the chair.

Becky reached for Shyster. Arthur stopped her. "Wait," he said.

"He's going to hurt him!" Becky shrugged Arthur's hand off her shoulder.

"Give them a chance."

With his black back arched and his tail swollen to twice its size, Shyster spat at Toby. The kitten didn't move; his blank green eyes stared up curiously at the bigger cat.

A low, piercing wail came out of Shyster. It was the sound cats made in the alley. Becky grabbed him. "No," she said. "No!"

Shyster squirmed out of her arms. Grumbling, he stalked out of the room, with his tail held high.

Becky watched him leave. "Why's he being so mean?"

"That's how cats get to know one another," Arthur said, "especially two males. They'll get used to each other. Don't worry."

From the second floor landing came another

long thin wail. It reminded Becky of going home.

After supper, Becky filled an old blue bowl with dry cat food. She left it on the kitchen counter and went to look for Shyster. Toby was asleep in the big cat's favorite chair. He yawned and stretched when she touched his back.

Becky checked under the couch in the living room. There were a couple of silver balls, but no black cat. "Shyster," she shouted, "here, Shyster."

He wasn't in her room or behind the toilet bowl where he often hid from the heat. She found him in a closet under the basement stairs.

Becky crawled into the small space and sat cross-legged on the stone floor. It was damp and cool, leaning against the cement wall. Shyster whined when she scooped him into her lap. "Don't be mad at me. I love you." She nuzzled his ear. "It's all Arthur's fault. He said you needed a friend 'cause you're lonely. I didn't know you'd hate Toby."

By the time Becky carried Shyster up to the kitchen, he was purring. She gave him food and leaned on the counter watching him eat.

The phone rang in the front hall, and Becky picked it up. "Hello?"

"It's Martha. I can't come over. My mother says it's too late now."

"Aww, too bad. What are you doing tomorrow?"

"I have to mow. If you come over, I could teach you to drive a tractor."

"Are you kidding!"

"It's not hard, Becky."

"You think I could?"

"Sure, why not?"

"My father always talked about driving tractors when he was a kid."

"Did he grow up on a farm?"

"No, he just spent a couple of summers visiting one."

"Well, come over early. We have to cut the grass before it gets hot."

"Okay. Listen, Martha?"

"Yeah?"

"I might have to bring Toby back."

"Why?"

"I'm afraid Shyster is going to hurt him."

"He won't."

"You don't know what's been going on around here."

Just then Becky heard a strange noise in the

kitchen. "I gotta go. See you tomorrow." She ran towards the kitchen.

Scared, Becky hesitated in the doorway. There was Toby with one gray paw in Shyster's blue bowl. And Shyster was growling. When the kitten didn't move, Shyster cuffed him. Toby backed away, circled the bowl, and tried from the other side. Shyster hissed, then he swatted Toby again. Toby didn't move.

Before it could happen again, Becky clapped her hands and shouted. "Shyster, no!"

Both cats jumped. Toby's leg hit the lip of the bowl, flipping it. The bowl clattering against the floor sent the cats running in different directions. Dry cat food lay scattered on the white linoleum. "You guys are too much," Becky said shaking her head.

She was almost finished picking up when the screen door opened and slammed shut. Becky saw her mother's sandals and Arthur's boots standing in the kitchen doorway.

"They still giving each other a hard time?" Arthur chuckled.

Becky tossed the last of the food into the bowl and stood up. Wiping her hands on her jeans, she said, "Shyster almost bashed Toby's brains in. I'm afraid he'll kill him."

Mrs. Rader glanced at Arthur. "He wouldn't, would he?"

Arthur shook his head. "No," he said in a more serious tone. "If Shyster wanted to kill Toby, he would have by now. Animals don't worry about being polite."

"Yeah, but he really hit him," Becky said.

Arthur put his wide hands on her shoulders. He looked down at her. "I know this'll sound crazy, but they're playing. You just have to let them do their cat stuff."

Becky pulled away. "Listen, Arthur, I'm not letting Shyster kill that kitten." She left before Arthur could say any more.

Later, Mrs. Rader turned off the lamp in Becky's room. When she sat on the edge of the bed, moonlight cut across her face and shoulders. "Becky, I don't like the way you're acting toward Arthur."

"He doesn't care about Toby."

"I don't think that's true."

"Maybe Shyster hates Toby." Becky pulled the covers up over her shoulders. "How does Arthur know?"

"He's lived around animals all his life. He's probably seen them do this before."

"You know something!" Becky kicked her covers off. "I hate the way he's always being nice to me. He's never going to be my father."

"Oh honey, he's not trying to. No one ever could."

"Well, tell him that!"

"I'm sure he knows. And besides how do you want him to act? Nasty and mean? Lock you up in an old dark cellar and throw away the key?"

Becky tried not to smile. "Okay, okay, I know he's not a troll."

Mrs. Rader smiled. "You might even say something to Arthur. I know he'd understand."

"Like what?"

"That you miss your father, still."

Becky looked down at her hands. What her mother suggested sounded hard. "He knows anyway," she said.

"What makes you say that?"

"Martha overheard him."

"So then if it's not Arthur, what's bothering you?"

Becky shrugged. "I don't know—I ..." She tried to think how to say what she felt. "I don't understand how Daddy could go away—that's all."

Mrs. Rader fingered the old-fashioned lace on the pillow. "I don't either, not really. All I know is, he decided he had to. Maybe someday we'll figure out why."

Talking about her father made her mother look sad. Becky changed the subject. "Momma, did Arthur's sister die?"

Startled, Mrs. Rader said, "Well, yes, how'd you hear?"

"Martha told me. What happened?"

"She had weak kidneys. Nobody knew till it was too late."

"How old was she?"

"Nine or ten. Why?"

"I was just wondering."

"Does it bother you, sleeping here?"

"No. What was her name?"

"Barbara. Ask Arthur. He'll tell you about her."

They both heard the floor boards creak out in the hall. Becky thought it was Arthur, but a small gray paw wrapped itself around the bottom of the door. Toby pushed his way into her room. He stood in the moonlight, ears laid back, expecting danger. Then he jumped on Becky's bed.

"Hi, Toby," she whispered. "Where's Shyster, Momma?"

"Downstairs."

Toby jumped over the hills Becky's feet made out of the covers. He settled in a tight ball near the back of her knees.

Becky stroked the warm gray fur. "He's so cute; I don't want to take him back."

Toby rolled over with his legs in the air, white belly exposed. His purring had a soft wheezing sound to it.

"Maybe you won't have to. Give them some more time."

"If Toby goes, I want to go home too."

"Let's decide on Saturday. By then we'll have been here almost two weeks."

Under the covers, Becky counted her fingers. That was three more days.

"Maybe by then Shyster and Toby will be buddies." Mrs. Rader leaned over and kissed Becky. "Good night, sweets," she said.

After her mother was gone, Becky slipped out of bed. She stood in the doorway to her room. "Shyster," she whispered. "Here, Shyster."

There was no answer. Nothing moved.

Becky tiptoed down the stairs past the kitchen where her mother and Arthur were sitting. She checked under the couch and in the basement closet, but Shyster was nowhere to be found that night.

CHAPTER 7

Thursday morning, Becky found Martha behind the Ryans' house in an old shed. Inside the wooden building all kinds of farm machinery and tools were crowded together. Martha finished filling the small red tractor with gasoline.

"All set for your driving lesson?" She rested the silver can on top of the tractor.

"Don't you need a license?"

"Nope. All the kids around here drive them."

"And it's okay?"

"Yup. You can't drive the regular roads, just on private land." Martha put the can on a shelf.

"Well, all right, if you say so. But could I watch you for a while?"

"Sure, just let me back it out."

Becky waited outside while Martha climbed onto the tractor and started the engine. It was so noisy that she couldn't hear Martha as the tractor moved backwards. "What?" she shouted.

"I said," Martha said, still yelling as the engine noise died, "you'll have to sit between my legs."

"Will we both fit behind the wheel?"

"Sure. Now, this is the brake. Watch how I can always stop."

It took Martha a lot of explaining and Becky a lot of questions before they were both ready to try riding on the tractor together. Finally, Becky knew how to turn the engine on and off, how to make the tractor move slow or fast and how to go in reverse.

When they took off, Becky sat on the front edge of the seat and Martha on the back. Martha let Becky control the brake, and slowly Martha steered them out onto the open field to begin the mowing.

The sun was warm, and the sky was clear as they circled the field for the first time. Once the tractor began cutting, the sweet smell of hay rose up all around them.

"This is great," Becky shouted. "I love it." She leaned back against Martha with her eyes closed and let her head fill up with the sounds and smells. Even with her eyes shut, she could see the field in her mind.

"You want to try it alone?" Martha's question jolted Becky out of her daydreaming.

With only a little hesitation, Becky said, "Okay."

Martha stood close by when Becky started up the tractor. And for a little while she ran behind Becky to make sure she was all right. But after Becky made it partway across the field, she was on her own.

She was careful to avoid the large rocks and not to come too close to the wild berry bushes. She made big circles around the trees the same way Martha had. After two more times, Becky stopped near the stone wall where Martha was sitting.

"Had enough?" Martha shouted.

"No, I want you to ride it with me. That was best."

Martha climbed on behind Becky. She took over the brake, and Becky handled the steering. Sometimes they made the small tractor go fast, and other times they slowed it down to a crawl.

"Close your eyes," Becky shouted.

"Why?" Martha shouted back.

"Just try it. It's fun."

By midmorning they had finished the entire field in front of the Ryans' house. Becky's nose and cheeks were a rosy pink when she followed Martha inside for lunch.

"I really have to go. My mother said three o'clock." Becky cut across the field.

"I'll walk you partway." Martha kept up with her.

"Are you going to sleep over tonight?" Becky asked Martha as they reached the woods.

"I don't know if I can. It's my brother's birthday. How about tomorrow or Saturday?"

Becky took a deep breath then blurted out her words. "I might not be here by Saturday. My mother and I could be back in the city by then."

Martha stopped short on the path. "How come?"

Becky shrugged and looked at the muddy ground.

"Aren't you having a good time? I thought you were."

Becky studied Martha's sneakers with the hole near her big toe. "Yeah, I am. It's just that . . ."

"Doesn't your mother like Arthur any more?"

Becky shook her head. "It's not that."

"So?"

"I miss my father. I want to go back."

Martha sat down on a rock. She picked up a stick and broke off the dead twigs. "I was hoping you'd stay and we'd be in the same classes at school."

Becky watched Martha draw lines in the soft dirt. She thought of them driving the tractor that morning. "We would come back to visit you."

Martha nodded, not looking up. "It wouldn't be like now."

Becky knew Martha was right. It wouldn't be the same.

"Couldn't you miss him and stay here?"

"What do you mean?"

"You don't have to be in the city to miss your father."

"Arthur might not let me see him if I stay here."

Martha threw the stick aside. "Oh, come on! He'd never do that." She stood up and thrust her hands in her front pockets. "I can't believe you."

Becky took a step backwards. "What do you mean?"

"Arthur's really nice. He'd never do that."

"Well, he might."

"That's just not true, and you know it! Listen, I have to go." Martha shoved aside a fat shrub.

Becky watched Martha disappear between the green bushes. "Hey, Martha, wait."

"Yeah?" Martha turned back slowly.

Becky didn't know what to say. "I'll call you later. Okay?"

Martha didn't answer.

CHAPTER 8

"Ouch!" Becky said when the pin pricked her knee.

Her mother spit out the mouthful of straight pins. "Sorry. Now don't move, so I can fix the hem."

Becky fidgeted with her braids while her mother crawled around on the floor. Mrs. Rader was trying to make the front and back hem even. "Hold still, Becky."

"Are you almost done?"

"Yes. What's wrong? You're really grumpy."

"Nothing," Becky mumbled. "It's just hot with this on."

"Well, at least you're going to have one new dress for school."

The mention of school reminded Becky of going home. "Where are Shyster and Toby? I didn't see them when I came in the front door."

"Downstairs. You know, I think they're getting along better. I was watching them for a little while. Okay," she stood up, "you're all set. Just take it off carefully."

Moments later Becky reached the bottom of the stairs. She found the cats racing around the house. Shyster was being stampeded down the hall by the kitten. "Oh yeah, a whole lot better."

She expected to find them on the back porch, but the screen door had been propped open with a broom. Outside the cats charged across the lawn. "Arthur, you jerk!" She halted in the doorway.

Toby ran up one tree, jumped down and ran for another. Shyster lay collapsed in the grass.

Becky could hear him panting as she crossed the grass. "Shyster. Toby." When they saw her coming, they bolted into the bushes.

Becky stamped her feet on every step up to

the second floor. She pushed open the door to her mother's room. "I hate it here!"

Mrs. Rader turned away from the sewing machine. "What's wrong?"

"Arthur left the door open and—"

"No, the cats were driving me crazy. They were begging to go outside. So I decided to leave the door open."

"But," Becky's voice shook, "they might run away."

"They've been going in and out of the house all day."

"They just went into the woods. If they don't come back, how will I find them?"

"Remember what Arthur said about animal instinct?" Mrs. Rader crossed the room.

"You're on his side, now."

"Becky, you can't keep them caged up. You have to trust that they'll come home."

"But suppose they get run over or someone steals them?"

Mrs. Rader put her arms around Becky and pulled her close. "You're having a hard time letting them out, aren't you?"

"Yeah," Becky said. "How come everybody goes away from me?"

"What do you mean?"

"First Daddy and now the cats."

Mrs. Rader rested her chin on the top of Becky's head. "You still have me."

Becky didn't answer. Instead, she buried her head against her mother's side.

"Going away," Mrs. Rader said, "is a part of life. You just have to love people or cats extra hard when they're with you. And maybe they'll stay, but sometimes they don't."

"Are you going to leave me, too?"

"No, Becky, I'm staying. I don't want to go away from you."

Becky closed her eyes and took a deep breath. She could smell the soap her mother used. She stayed like that for a long time, trying hard not to think about Martha or the cats or her father or Arthur.

Later, Becky stood looking out the window in her room. Even though her mother had said not to worry about the cats, Becky couldn't get them out of her mind. Outside, the old apple tree that didn't grow apples anymore blocked part of the view. The cats were nowhere to be seen.

Becky noticed her father's old scout book on the shelf, and it gave her an idea. Maybe she could find cat tracks in the woods. If she brought treats, they might follow her back. She grabbed the book and headed down the stairs.

Outside, it was muggy. "Shyster, Toby," she called.

The woods were quiet in the late afternoon heat. Nothing moved.

She found a few prints down near the stream where the dirt was soft. None of them were made by cat paws. And there was nothing anywhere else. Becky looked for black and gray fur that might have caught on low bushes. Her father's book said trackers checked for that also.

It was no use. There was no way she could find them. Just like her father, the cats were gone. Becky sat alone in the woods, not wanting to go inside.

"Pass the salad please," Arthur said to Becky in a low voice.

Becky nudged the dish over the table. She kept her eyes on her nearly full plate.

Only when they heard scratching at the screen door did Becky look up. It was Shyster. "Where *were* you?" she asked, letting him in.

Shyster sauntered into the kitchen. He began whining as soon as he saw his empty blue bowl. Becky opened a package of food.

Outside there was a terrible yowling. "What's that?" It sounded to Becky like a baby screaming.

"I'll see." Arthur headed towards the front of the house.

Becky heard him open the door and then laugh. "Well," he said, coming back down the hall. "We're glad you could finally make it. Look who's here, Becky."

Becky breathed a sigh of relief when she saw Arthur talking to Toby. She picked up the kitten's bowl to wash.

Snarls and hissing broke out behind her. "Shyster—no!" She turned around.

But it wasn't Shyster's fault. The little kitten had started it. Gray and black fur floated into the air as the cats rolled and tumbled across the kitchen floor.

Becky grabbed for them, but Arthur yanked her back. "Now, stay out of that." His voice was sharp.

"But Shyster's bigger. He'll hurt Toby!"

"No, he won't!"

"I'm taking him back to Martha's," Becky

shouted at Arthur. "If you don't care about him getting killed, I do."

"Now, listen here, Becky." Arthur's narrow face flushed with color. "They will work it out!"

Just then a fierce yowl broke out of Toby. With his ears laid flat against his head, he went racing through the kitchen door. Shyster tore after him.

Becky looked at her mother. "I want to go home. You said we could."

She shoved past Arthur. "Shyster! Toby!"

They were on the back porch. Shyster had stretched out in his favorite chair, with his face towards the back cushions. His breathing came in short gasps.

Toby crouched under the chair. His eyes followed Shyster's tail, which hung over the edge of the seat.

"You guys." Becky threw herself onto the wicker couch. "You've got to cut it out."

The cats ignored her. Shyster flicked his tail. Toby batted it deliberately.

Becky didn't move. "You're really asking for it, Toby. He's going to let you have it."

Shyster twitched his long black tail again. The kitten swatted it. The larger cat jumped down. They lay nose to nose on the floor.

"Come on, guys," Becky said, but she kept still when Shyster reached out and cuffed the kitten.

Toby's gray paw batted Shyster back. Shyster was still. Then Toby crept out from under his hiding place and flopped down close to him. In less than a second, Shyster began licking the kitten's head.

Becky couldn't believe what she was seeing. There was Shyster bathing Toby, and they were both purring. "Will you two please make up your minds! Are you friends or enemies?"

Toby rolled over. His little pink tongue washed Shyster's wide black back.

Becky was on her way upstairs to her mother's room, but she stopped in the hall. "Arthur?" She knocked on the study door. "Can I come in?"

"Yes."

Becky pushed open the door. Arthur was sitting with his feet up on his desk. "I just wanted to tell you . . ."

"Yes?" He looked up from the book on his lap.

"That the cats are . . . are being okay."

Arthur swung his legs to the floor. "Thank goodness!"

"I'm sorry I got angry."

Arthur stood up. "No, that's okay. I shouldn't have yelled. I knew you didn't understand what they were doing."

"I was scared they'd . . ."

"I know."

"You're not mad?"

"Of course not, Becky. You didn't do anything wrong."

Becky studied the pattern in the carpet. She couldn't look at Arthur.

He rested his calloused hands on her shoulders. "I kept insisting they'd be friends so you'd stay."

"You really want us to?"

"Yes, Becky, I really do."

"Arthur." Becky took a deep breath. "I still miss my father, but I'm going to tell my mother I want to stay."

Arthur squeezed Becky's shoulders. "I think we need a celebration. Let's go buy some ice cream."

"Okay." Becky finally looked up at him. She could tell he was happy.

"We could get Martha on our way," Arthur said, as they entered the hall.

"I'll call her."

Arthur ran up the stairs.

She knew the Ryans' number by heart. While the phone rang, Becky wondered if Martha and she might be in the same class at school.

"Hello?"

"Martha, it's me."

"Yeah?"

From Martha's tone, Becky could tell her friend was still upset. "Listen, you were right about you-know-who."

"Becky, what are you talking about?"

"You want to go get some ice cream with me and Arthur and come here after?"

"Sure. But what were you just talking about?"

"I'll tell you later. Oh—and Martha, we're not going back to the city."

"Why didn't you say so? That's great! What made you change your mind?"

"I'll tell you on the way. You're not still angry, are you?"

"Not anymore."

"See you in five minutes." Becky hung up the phone.

"What was that all about?" Mrs. Rader came down the stairs behind Arthur.

Becky smiled. "Martha was real upset 'cause I said we might be going home."

Arthur burst out laughing. "She's not the only one."

Later, the four of them were sitting around the kitchen table. Becky slipped her empty ice cream bowl under the table without Mrs. Rader or Arthur noticing. She winked at Martha.

"I'm pretty sure," Arthur said, "we can get all of your furniture onto Ryans' pickup truck. And if not, we'll make two trips."

Mrs. Rader put down her spoon. "I'll need a few days to get everything packed and tell my principal I'm not coming back to teach."

Arthur leaned against his chair and folded his arms. "You give me a call when you're ready, and I'll drive in."

"It's hard to believe." Mrs. Rader looked from Arthur to Becky. "There're only two weeks left till school starts."

"Do you think," Becky said, still watching the cats, "Martha and I will be in the same class?"

"Good chance." Arthur nodded.

Mrs. Rader pushed away from the table. "I

wonder how long it will take me to find a teaching job here."

"I don't know," Arthur said, "it's a small system."

"Maybe I should try something else."

"It's okay with me if you don't want to work."

Mrs. Rader shook her head. "No, I'd rather be busy."

Becky looked up from the cats. "Once you said you'd love to sew all day. Maybe you could do that."

"Of course," Arthur agreed. "Open a dress shop! You can have the downstairs study. I'll help you set it up."

Mrs. Rader laughed. "That's one way to get rid of all the material I have. I'll have to think about that when we go back to the apartment."

"Good idea, Becky." Arthur patted her shoulder.

"Momma, would it be okay if Martha came back with us?"

"If you two promise to help with the packing."

"Oh, wow, I'd love to." Martha beamed. "I've never been to a big city."

"We'll help," Becky said to her mother. And to Martha, she said, "But I'll have to introduce you to my friend Iris and show you the zoo. Hey—what will we do about the cats?"

"I'll take care of them." Arthur glanced towards the floor. "But I might have to put Shyster on a diet."

Mrs. Rader leaned over the side of her chair. "And I'm not sure that ice cream is going to be part of his daily program." She lifted Shyster onto her lap.

Shyster curled up into a sleek black ball and allowed himself to be stroked. His purring was a rumble.

"I'm glad you talked me into taking him Becky." Mrs. Rader scratched his chin as she spoke. "He's become a wonderful friend."

Becky smiled. Toby was curled up on her left foot underneath the table. He was purring, too.

PART 3

CHAPTER 9

It was a bright October afternoon when Becky biked home from school. She dropped her bicycle outside near the porch. "Momma? I'm home," Becky yelled as she hurried through the kitchen. "Momma?"

"Up here." Mrs. Rader stood at the top of the stairs. "You have to hurry. I told Mrs. Ryan I'd set up while she's out with Martha."

"Okay, but I still have to wrap Martha's present."

"I'll do that while you're getting changed."

"I'm wearing my red jumper."

"Fine." Mrs. Rader started down the stairs then stopped. "Did Martha say anything in school today?"

"No, and everyone was being very careful not to give it away. I think the party is really going to surprise her."

"Wonderful. I'll see you in five minutes, downstairs. I'll need some help getting the cake and salads in the car."

In her room Toby was sprawled out on the bed. Becky popped a tin foil ball at him. Toby pounced. Becky watched him bat it around the quilt as she changed into the dress her mother had made.

"Where's Shyster?" Becky looked in the closet, but he wasn't among her shoes and sneakers. She began combing her hair.

"Shyster?" Becky called out again as she started down the stairs. He didn't come when she rattled the bag of cat treats. He's probably in the closet downstairs, Becky thought. That was where he'd been hiding lately.

Toby rubbed against her legs, and Becky gave him an extra handful of food. "Okay for you, Shyster. I'll see you guys later."

Becky shut the kitchen door behind her. The

air was crisp and clear as she climbed into the car.
And the mountains at the far end of the meadow
were red and orange.

When Becky and her mother pulled up the driveway later that evening. Arthur was waiting for
them. He came down the porch steps and opened
the door on Becky's side.

"Hi!" Becky got out. "We brought you a
piece of birthday cake."

Arthur was quiet for a moment looking at
Becky and her mother. "Becky," he said leaning
on the car. "Shyster is sick. I was just getting
ready to call Ryans' house."

"What do you mean?" Becky felt her throat
tighten.

"He wasn't around all afternoon, so I went
looking for him. I found him in the downstairs
closet but way far back. He wouldn't come out. I
had to crawl in there to get him."

"What's wrong?"

"I don't know, but he doesn't seem able to
move."

"Where is he?" Becky's voice shook.

"I have him wrapped in a blanket on the front seat of my car. The vet said she would take a look at him."

"We'll all go," Mrs. Rader said quickly. "Come on."

Becky sat in the front seat with Shyster in her lap. He mewed once but hardly moved all the way into town. "It's okay, Shyster. You're going to be all right." Becky stroked his head.

The back door to the vet's house had a light on when they pulled up. A lady in a green surgical shirt opened the door. "Hello," she said, "I'm Dr. Huntington. Come this way." Shyster whined when the doctor took him in her arms.

They followed her through the back end of the house and into her front offices. Very carefully she put the cat on a silver topped table.

Becky took her mother's hand. Standing as close to Shyster as she could, Becky watched as the doctor began an examination.

"What's his name?" said the doctor without looking up.

"Shyster," Becky said.

After a few minutes Dr. Huntington took off the stethoscope. "How long have you had him?"

Mrs. Rader answered. "Since July. He's a stray that Becky found in an alley."

"I'm afraid he's very very sick. There's something wrong with his heart. From the way it's racing, I would guess it's enlarged."

"What's that?" Becky's voice cracked.

"It means his heart was not strong enough when he was born to get the blood to his whole body. So it has to pump harder. Then the heart usually becomes larger and out of shape to cope with the extra work."

"But he's never been sick."

Dr. Huntington nodded. "It doesn't show up till it's too late. Doctors rarely check for it in cats."

"Can't you give him medicine?"

Dr. Huntington had a very sad look on her face when she shook her head. "Come around the other side of me, Becky. I want to show you something."

Becky let go of her mother's hand. She watched the doctor open Shyster's mouth very gently.

"See, his gums are all white? That means the blood is not getting there. He can't move his legs either. Shyster's heart has become very weak."

"Oh, Shyster," Becky whispered.

Dr. Huntington looked at Becky's mother and Arthur. "I think it would be best if we put him to sleep. He's in a lot of pain, and this will end it quickly.''

Becky reached for her mother. ''I don't want him to die. Isn't there anything that would help him?''

''There are some experimental drugs that shock the heart,'' the doctor said to all three of them. ''But I don't want to try them. I'm afraid he'd be paralyzed from lack of blood now, even if he did live. And I doubt very much that he would.''

Becky looked at Shyster stretched out on the silver slab table. ''But we haven't had him long enough.''

''Chances are,'' Dr. Huntington said, ''that if you hadn't adopted him, he might have died sooner. Sick animals don't last long on their own. You've probably lengthened his life by taking care of him.''

''He was really scrawny when we first found him,'' Mrs. Rader said.

''In the wild, we know that stronger animals will take food away from weaker ones. That might have been happening to him.''

Becky couldn't take her eyes off Shyster. ''Will it hurt him?''

"No. But you can wait in the other room while I give him the shot if you'd like."

Becky began to cry. "I want to stay with Shyster."

"Are you sure Becky?" Mrs. Rader put an arm around her.

Becky nodded her head. But she couldn't watch when Dr. Huntington gave Shyster the injection.

She held him for the last few moments before he died. He felt heavy in her arms, and his black fur was soft. He mewed weakly, just once, and then it seemed as if he had fallen asleep.

"You're a very brave girl," Dr. Huntington said as she led them outside. She kept her hand on Becky's shoulder till they reached the car.

Arthur spoke quietly as they drove back home. "We should bury him right away. I could dig a hole under the apple tree that's near your window, Becky. Then you could look out and think about him sometimes."

Becky said nothing. She held Shyster

wrapped in the soft blue blanket on her lap. She didn't say a word when they pulled up to the house, but she followed Arthur across the front lawn and around the side to the apple tree.

Only when the shovel began to grate against the rocky soil, did Becky say, "I want to help. I want to dig some of the hole, too."

The ground came away easily as Becky made the hole deeper. She could smell the moist, tangy dirt, as she heaped it up next to the hole. Even though she was sad, Becky felt good about where she was putting Shyster.

The shovel clanged on a rock. Becky leaned her body against the wooden handle to pry the rock free. Her hands ached from the strain. There was mud on her red dress. The earth groaned and sighed, but finally the rock broke free.

"Save the rocks," Arthur said, picking one up. "We'll pile them up on top so nothing disturbs Shyster."

"It'll be a marker," Mrs. Rader said.

"Here," Becky handed the shovel to Arthur. "I'll be right back."

It was dark in the living room, but Becky knew her way around without turning on the lights. She felt under the couch. Shyster's toys were against the back wall. She shoved them into her pocket and went outside.

It was completely dark when they placed Shyster, wrapped in a blanket, in his grave. Becky dropped the silver balls beside him. Arthur filled the hole up. Becky and her mother put the heavy boulders on top.

Becky placed the last of the rocks over Shyster. She was dizzy and sick to her stomach from crying. And she felt as if everything she loved was disappearing.

In the middle of the night, Becky awoke from a deep sleep. There was something bad in her dreams that she didn't want to remember. Her feet were cold. She tried to find a warm spot under the covers. A strong breeze was blowing in from the open window.

When she got up to close it, Becky saw the pile of stones in the side yard. The bad thing was not in her dream but outside. "Shyster, are you scared," Becky whispered. "Does it hurt?"

She dressed quickly and went outside. The night was chilly and the grass wet. Her sneakers were soaked by the time she reached the stones under the apple tree.

Becky lay down next to the stones. She wanted to curl up with them, but they were cold and hard. "Shyster, are you there? I can't feel you."

The stones were silent. The ground was silent. Only the night wind whispered to the trees. It said nothing to Becky.

"Becky?" a voice said. "Becky."

Frightened, she looked up. Where did the voice come from? Who used her name? She glanced over her shoulder. Arthur was coming across the lawn.

"I couldn't sleep," he said.

Becky was glad it was him and not something spooky.

"Could I sit with you? I've been thinking about Shyster all night."

"Okay." She leaned against the rock pile.

They sat in silence watching a half moon swim in and out of gray-white clouds. The smell of newly turned soil floated up from the cold earth.

Becky whispered, "I don't know where he is."

"No one understands what happens after

death. But when I was young, my dog got killed. The morning we buried him, Ryan told me I could find Butch's spirit if I looked into the eyes of other dogs.''

"Did you?''

"I saw it flickering in another dog, years later.''

"You think Shyster's has gone into another cat already?''

"I don't know, Becky.''

"Maybe I'll see Shyster's spirit, too.''

"You might.'' Arthur leaned against the rock pile also.

"Does the same thing happen when people die?''

"I have a funny feeling it does. 'Cause every once in a while I hear my brother's voice and it sounds just like my father's.''

Becky sat thinking. "I wonder if you have to be dead. You think it could happen when people are still alive?''

"You mean a part of a person's living spirit entering another?''

"Yeah.''

"I don't know. I never heard of that before.''

Becky stared up through the apple tree at the sky. Even though it was still dark, the birds were beginning to chatter and chirp and caw. "It's almost morning," she said.

"We should go in and get something hot to drink."

Becky stood up with Arthur. He put his arm around her, and they headed back across the lawn.

CHAPTER 10

A few days later, Becky and her mother were in the basement. Becky slammed the clothes dryer door shut. "I keep thinking Shyster'll just come around a corner," she said.

"I keep forgetting, too." Mrs. Rader turned the dials on the washing machine. "It'll take us some time, I guess."

A long, piercing wail startled them. "Was that Toby?" Mrs. Rader looked around the room.

"It sounded like Shyster."

There was a second cry. This time they knew it came from inside the closet. Becky opened the door. She crawled inside.

At first she couldn't see a thing. But as her eyes adjusted to the dimness, she made out a form. There was another cry.

"Becky? What is it?"

Becky backed out of the closet and stood up. "Momma, it's Toby."

"Is he hurt?"

"No, he's just sitting in Shyster's spot in the closet. Do you think he knows Shyster is dead?"

"I don't know if that's possible."

Toby bolted out of the closet and up the stairs. Becky followed him up to the back porch. He jumped into Shyster's chair. "What's the matter, pal?"

Toby dropped to the floor. Pacing in front of the door, he whined at Becky.

"I think he wants to go looking for Shyster," Becky said to her mother.

"Poor thing." Mrs. Rader stood in the kitchen doorway. "He really does seem to be upset."

"Momma, what if something bad happens to him?"

"Sometimes, Becky, you have to take chances."

Becky hesitated in front of the door. The

small gray cat scratched at the sill. He looked up at Becky and whined again.

"I know it's really not fair to keep you in," she said to the cat. "But it's hard to let you go." Slowly Becky opened the screen door. She didn't stay to watch him run into the woods.

When Arthur came home, Becky told him about the strange thing that had happened. Arthur peeled potatoes while he listened. "He was used to Shyster. They were buddies."

"It was so spooky," Becky said as she set the table. "Like he really knew."

Mrs. Rader tossed the salad. "I think it was his own way of saying good-bye to Shyster."

"He needs a pal." Arthur turned the flame up under the water. "Just as Shyster did."

Later when Martha called about the math homework, Becky told her what had happened. "It was like Toby was really searching for Shyster."

"He's never been alone. He always had his brothers and sisters around him in the barn."

"I wonder if Toby really misses Shyster."

"I don't know, but cats like to sleep all heaped up together. Maybe that's what he wants."

"You have any kittens left?"

"Sure, Leda's. You want one?"

"No, I was just wondering."

"Well, I'll see you tomorrow, right?"

"Yes." Becky hung up the phone. Not long after, she heard Toby scratching at the back door.

Martha was out on the back porch the next morning when Becky and her mother drove up. "The cats are in the barn," she said coming down the steps. "Want to see them before we go?"

"Yes, let's." Mrs. Rader put her arm around Becky's shoulders. Martha led the way.

"I'm only looking," Becky told her mother.

The litter was tucked into a bale of hay not far from an open window. Three kittens were left, two spotted orange ones and a long-haired tan-and-white.

"Oh, wow, are you cute." Becky lifted up the squirmy tan bundle. The cat shifted and twisted in her arms.

"That's Ebert," Martha said. "He's not used to being held."

Becky stroked the wide fluffy tail. "What a fatty."

"You'd see he's skinny if he got wet," Martha said.

Mrs. Rader tickled his chin. "I can't believe no one wanted him."

Ebert jumped out of Becky's arms and ran back to the litter with his tail in the air. He plopped down with a grunt.

Becky laughed. "He's great."

"Why don't you take him?"

Becky looked at her mother. "You think I should?"

"Yes," Mrs. Rader and Martha said together.

Becky squatted down beside the kitten washing himself. "Hey, Ebert." He purred when she stroked the top of his head. "Yeah," she said, "I really like him."

On the way back from town, Mrs. Rader and Becky dropped Martha off. And they took Ebert with them. Ebert disappeared over the seat of the car, to explore the back end. Becky watched as he climbed into a box of old clothes and sniffed his way around.

Mrs. Rader slowed down at the intersection. "Ebert's going to be fun."

"I was thinking about Shyster. I feel bad."

"How come?"

"Maybe I shouldn't have gotten Ebert."

"I don't understand."

"It's like I'm getting rid of Shyster."

"Replacing him, you mean?"

"Yeah."

"You're really not. You can go on loving Shyster even if he is dead. Having Ebert doesn't mean you have to stop."

"That's what it feels like."

"In your heart, you're not getting rid of Shyster. You're just going on being alive."

"I feel so sad."

"I know. But there was nothing else we could do."

"Maybe we shouldn't have put him to sleep."

"He was already dying. There was no other way." Mrs. Rader pulled the car up the driveway.

They sat for a moment listening to the engine quiet down. Ebert jumped back over the front seat and settled in Becky's lap. She stroked his wide flat head. After a while Becky said, "Daddy's never coming home again, is he?"

"You might see him someday."

"But he's never coming back to live with us. Just like Shyster."

"You're right, never like that." Mrs. Rader looked out the window. When she turned to

Becky, there were tears in her eyes. "In a way Shyster and your father were the same."

"How?"

"I think of them as wild things who didn't stay long."

Becky nodded, petting the cat in her lap. He was biting on her thumb with sharp, prickly teeth.

She opened the car door. Ebert squirmed and wiggled as she carried him up the walk to the house.

"Just think,"—Mrs. Rader held open the screen door to the porch—"how happy Toby is going to be to have company again."

Becky stopped short. She turned and grinned at her mother. "No, I bet he'll be really angry."

Surprised, her mother laughed. "You know, you're right. He's going to hate him."

"Here we go again," Becky giggled as she put Ebert on the floor. The tan and white kitten headed for Toby's food dish. "Hey, Toby," Becky yelled. "There's someone here to see you."

CHAPTER 11

The mountains had disappeared behind an all white sky. Snow covered the ground, and the trees looked like lace doilies. Arthur was driving Becky home from school.

"You'd think by now," Becky said, "Toby and Ebert would be friends."

"Oh, I think they are." Arthur smiled at her. "They just don't want you to know. Sooner or later, you'll catch them being nice to one another."

"Maybe," Becky said, "it's because they're around the same age. They're both kittens, really."

"Could be," Arthur said as he pulled into the driveway. "Listen, your mother and I are going over to Ryans' to pick out a Christmas tree. You want to come?"

"Yes, but I have to change and feed the cats." Becky collected her books and papers on the front seat.

"I just want to make sure we chop it down while there's still light."

Becky climbed out of the car. The cold air slapped her face and stung the inside of her nose. She paused for a moment to look at the apple tree. Beneath it snow had softened the pile of rocks. And all around the marker, the snow was decorated with bird tracks.

"Thinking about Shyster?" Arthur came around the car.

"I miss him."

"You probably always will."

"Arthur, do you still miss your sister?" Becky looked away from the rocks.

Arthur nodded, glancing at the white fields. When he spoke, Becky saw a cloud of steam escape from his lips. "She was my best friend. I have a hard time talking about her."

Becky nodded. She knew what he meant.

"Once in a while," she said, "I wish I had a sister. It seems like it would be fun."

"It was, lots. Sometimes when you're on the phone with Martha, it's as if Barbara's around again." Arthur flipped up his fur collar. "We better go in. It's freezing."

Becky thought about what Arthur said while she was changing her clothes. She hadn't known how to answer him.

Toby pushed open the door to her room. He jumped onto the bed and stretched out.

"Hi'ya fella." Becky scratched his white underbelly. Toby purred and nuzzled her arm.

Ebert waddled in and tried to jump up onto the bed. After several tries, he whined at Becky.

"I wouldn't get up there, if I were you Ebert." She smiled down at the tan kitten.

His yellow eyes blinked at Becky. He whined again more insistently.

"Okay." She bent to pick him up.

Toby hissed at the kitten standing at the end of the bed. Ebert moved cautiously toward the gray cat. When Toby cuffed Ebert, the younger cat didn't move.

"That wasn't very nice, Toby."

Becky began brushing her hair. In the mirror she could see Toby curled up on the bed. And there beside him was Ebert trying to snuggle.

Becky smiled. "You think you can always have things your way, Ebert?"

The cat grunted out a response.

With the brush still in her hand, Becky smiled at the mirror. Her thick brown hair was wavy like her father's. She had never noticed that before. It was like having a little of him within her.

"Come on, fellas. Food!"

Ebert took a flying leap off the bed. Toby hit the floor with a thud.

Just before she closed the door to her room, Becky spotted her father's old scouting book. Going down the stairs with it, she found her favorite section with the animal tracks. She left the book sitting open on Arthur's desk.

In the kitchen, Ebert had plopped in front of the blue bowl and wrapped his fat white paws around the base. Shyster used to do that, Becky thought as she dragged out the large bag of dry food.

"All set," Arthur came up the basement stairs. He closed the door behind him.

"Yup, just have to change their water."

Behind her Toby whined. He stood looking at Ebert eating.

"Looks like Toby wants a little something, too." Arthur pulled his jacket on. "I'll be warming up the car."

Becky filled another bowl for Toby and picked up her coat. She stood in the doorway watching. Toby moved over to the other bowl, and Ebert followed him.

Becky wasn't at all surprised when Toby swatted the kitten or when Ebert hissed back. Just before she opened the door to leave, they were rolling across the floor hissing and growling. "See you guys later!"

On the porch she struggled into her boots. In a couple of minutes, Becky knew, they'd probably be giving each other baths.

She closed the door and headed down the slippery walk. The sun was already sinking behind the snow-covered mountains. In the car, her mother and Arthur were waiting.